**W9-ASZ-383**

DATE DUE

| | | | |
|---|---|---|---|
| | | | |
| | | | |
| | | | |
| | | | |
| | | | |
| | | | |
| | | | |
| | | | |
| | | | |
| | | | |
| | | | |
| | | | |

# SOCCER 'CATS

#1

# The Captain Contest

## by Matt Christopher

### Illustrated by Daniel Vasconcellos

Little, Brown and Company

Boston   New York   London

## To Paul Christopher and Crystal Ann

First Edition

The characters and events portrayed in this book are fictitious. Any similarity to real persons, living or dead, is coincidental and not intended by the author.

Library of Congress Cataloging-in-Publication Data

Christopher, Matt.
    The captain contest / by Matt Christopher ; illustrated by Daniel Vasconcellos. — 1st ed.
        p.    cm. — (The Soccer Cats ; #1)
    Summary: Dewey loves to draw and wants to enter the soccer team logo contest, but he does not want to win the grand prize — being team captain.
    ISBN 0-316-14169-0
    [1. Soccer — Fiction.   2. Competition (Psychology) — Fiction.]
I. Vasconcellos, Daniel, ill.   II. Title.   III. Series: Christopher, Matt. Soccer Cats ; #1.
PZ7.C458Cap   1999
[Fic] — dc21                                                                98-33802

10   9   8   7   6   5   4   3   2   1

WOR

Printed in the United States of America

# Chapter 1

Ten-year-old Dewey London dragged behind his mother in the grocery store. Summer vacation had just started, and it was sunny outside. Trudging up and down aisles of food was not his idea of fun.

"Hey, Dewey!"

Dewey brightened when he saw his best buddy, Bundy Neel, coming toward him. Bundy, his dark hair sticking up as usual, didn't look thrilled to be in the store either.

"Man, my dad's taking forever to pick out cereal!" Bundy complained.

"Try listening to my mom talk about yogurt." Dewey stuck out his tongue and crossed his eyes. Bundy laughed.

"There's a display of beach toys up front," Bundy said. "Let's go hang out there."

The beach toy display was a disappointment. After five minutes, the boys were bored again. They wandered to the automatic exit doors and took turns jumping on the plastic matting to open them.

Just then, a fluorescent pink poster caught Dewey's eye.

"What's that?" he asked Bundy, tipping his baseball cap back to get a better look. They went over and read the poster.

SOCCER SIGN-UPS!
TEAMS FORMING NOW FOR A NEW
SUMMER LEAGUE

WHO? KIDS 9–12
WHEN? FRIDAY, JUNE 27,
FROM 9:00 A.M.–NOON
WHERE? JUNIOR HIGH GYMNASIUM

SPECIAL CONTEST: COME UP WITH
YOUR TEAM'S NAME AND T-SHIRT
LOGO, AND YOU'LL BE NAMED THE
CAPTAIN OF YOUR TEAM!

"Let's join!" Bundy said enthusiastically. "And we have to enter that contest. It would be so awesome to be team captain."

"You'd want to be team captain? Not me," Dewey said, shaking his head. The idea made him a little queasy.

Designing a team uniform, on the other hand, now *that* sounded cool. Dewey liked to draw and paint. Just last month, a painting he'd done won a prize in a school contest.

"Dewey! Bundy!" Mrs. London called to the boys from the checkout line.

4

"Time to get going, guys," Mr. Neel added.

Bundy tugged at Dewey's shirt. "Come on, let's tell them about the soccer league," he said.

Dewey listened as Bundy explained about the poster. Both parents agreed to bring the boys to the sign-ups.

"All right!" Bundy cried as they all left the store. "See you Friday, Dewey!"

Dewey waved. He helped load the groceries into the back of the car, then climbed in the front seat beside his mother. The whole time, his mind was turning over one question.

If he entered and won the logo design contest, would he *have* to be a team captain?

# Chapter 2

**O**n Friday morning, the junior high school gymnasium was crowded with kids waiting to sign up for the soccer league. Dewey spotted Bundy with two other boys, Alan Minter and Ted Gaddy. He hurried over to join them.

"Isn't this great?" Bundy said when Dewey reached them. "These guys are going to join, too. Let's make sure we all get on the same team."

"If we're not," Alan said, pushing his glasses back up his nose, "you better watch out for me on the field. I've been learning some fancy footwork from my sister." He faked a move around Bundy with a pretend ball.

"Speaking of sisters, here comes yours," Bundy said to Ted. Ted's twin sister, Lisa, appeared a moment later, her long brown ponytail bouncing behind her.

The five friends moved through the line together. One by one they added their names and addresses to the sign-up sheet at the table. They were all on Team Six, according to the sheet.

The woman behind the desk pointed to a stack of papers. "If you want to enter the uniform logo contest, be sure to take one of these rule sheets."

"That's for me!" Bundy said, grabbing a form. "Anyone else?"

Alan, Ted, and Lisa shook their heads. Dewey hesitated. Part of him really wanted to

try drawing the logo. But the thought of being team captain stopped him. He turned away from the table empty-handed.

Bundy grinned. "That makes it easier," he said happily. "Now we won't be in competition."

Dewey nodded along with the others, but something nagged him. He knew Bundy would make a good captain. Bundy always worked out who'd be on whose team when they played pick-up games, and nobody argued with his choices. On rainy days, he could always come up with a fun indoor game. Yep, Bundy was a natural leader.

But Dewey had sat next to Bundy in art class, so he knew Bundy couldn't draw worth beans. What sort of uniform logo could he possibly come up with?

These thoughts were whirling through Dewey's head as he left the gym with the others. Ted and Lisa lived just around the corner, so they took off right away. Alan's sister beeped her horn for him a moment later. Then Mr. Neel drove up.

"Hey, Dewey," Bundy called as he climbed into the car. "Let's meet at the field tomorrow for a game! I'll call everyone. Ten o'clock, okay?"

Dewey nodded and waved as the Neels drove away. Then he sat down on the curb to wait for his mother.

It was a breezy day. Dewey watched some dandelion fluff float by. He was just about to lie back onto the grass when he heard a shout.

Startled, he turned around. The woman from the sign-up table was frantically trying to catch some papers she'd dropped. The wind had scattered them all over the lawn.

Dewey sprang up to help. In a minute he had gathered a stack. He glanced down to see what they were.

His heart started pounding. He was holding copies of the contest rule sheets.

"Oh, thank you, young man," the woman

said. She held her hand out for Dewey's papers.

Dewey hesitated, then blurted out, "Could I have one of these?" Even as he said it, he felt a pang of guilt. What would Bundy say if he knew Dewey was thinking of entering the contest?

"Of course," the woman said, and took all but one rule sheet from him. Dewey folded the paper and was stuffing it into his back pocket just as his mother drove up.

"Dewey!" she called. "Sorry I'm late!"

Dewey hurried to the car and hopped in. The whole way home, the rule sheet seemed to burn a hole in his pocket.

# Chapter 3

**D**ewey put the rule sheet in his top desk drawer when he got home.

*Just because I have the rules,* he thought as he pushed the drawer shut, *doesn't mean I'm going to enter the contest.*

Another thought struck him. Maybe Bundy wasn't going to be the only one on the team to enter the contest. After all, there had been fifteen names on the list for Team Six. Just because Lisa, Ted, and Alan had said they weren't entering didn't mean someone else wasn't.

*I'll check around at the pick-up game tomorrow,* he decided before going to sleep that night. *If another kid on our team is entering the contest, then I will, too.*

"We weren't sure you were going to make it!" Bundy yelled the next day as Dewey hurried onto the field.

"We're going to play six-on-six," Bundy explained. "I put you on Lisa's team, okay?" Dewey nodded and joined his teammates.

Along with Lisa were her brother Ted, Jerry Dinh, Edith "Eddie" Sweeny, and Lou Barnes. Lou had only one good arm; the other was partially paralyzed. But that didn't slow him down one bit. In fact, he was the tallest, strongest kid there.

On Bundy's team were Alan Minter, Dale Tuget, Stookie Norris, Amanda Caler, and Roy Boswick.

Bundy's team had the ball first. Roy, a thin boy playing striker, toed it from center field to Stookie on his right. Stookie dribbled down the field. Amanda, a tiny but speedy girl, trotted behind him in the right halfback position. Bundy, in the other halfback slot, followed Roy. Alan hung back on defense, and Dale, a stocky boy with sandy brown hair, stood in the goal. Alan and Dale would swap back and forth during the game because neither really liked playing goalie.

As Stookie nosed the ball toward the opposing goal, freckle-faced Eddie Sweeny charged forward to meet him. Playing halfback, it was her job to make sure he couldn't take an easy shot on goal.

As the other halfback, Dewey followed the action carefully. When Stookie passed the ball back to Roy, Dewey shot forward and stole the ball!

"All right!" Dewey heard Ted yell from his place in goal. "Go, man, go!"

Dewey dribbled quickly downfield, then

looked for someone to pass to. Jerry and Lou were dancing near opposite sidelines, both eager to receive. Seeing Bundy start toward Jerry, Dewey booted a short pass to Lou.

Lou trapped it neatly. He spun around to begin the attack on goal.

*Crash!* He collided with Amanda, who had rushed to stop him. Stumbling, he lost his balance and fell to the ground right at Dewey's feet. The ball bounced over the sideline, out of bounds.

"Whoa!" Amanda cried. "Are you okay, Lou?"

Bundy and the rest of the kids hurried over. "Dewey, did you see what happened?" Bundy asked. "Was it tripping? If not, who touched it last?"

Both Amanda and Lou looked at Dewey expectantly. Dewey went tongue-tied, the way he always did in situations like this.

Then Amanda shrugged. "Well, I never

actually touched the *ball.* Just Lou. And he ran into me. So it should be our ball, I guess."

Bundy looked from Dewey to Lou, who was still sitting on the ground. "You okay with that?"

Lou hesitated, then nodded. Amanda retrieved the ball, and the rest of the kids scattered to their positions.

As he hurried back to his halfback spot, Dewey caught up to his fellow halfback, Eddie Sweeny.

"Hey, Eddie," he said, "I was wondering. Are you going to enter that logo contest?"

Eddie looked at Dewey with surprise, then understanding. "Oh, that's right, you were late today. So you missed it when we decided Bundy should be Team Six captain. We all agreed not to enter so he'd win for sure."

Dewey swallowed his disappointment. "Oh" was all he said.

Yet he knew Bundy was the best choice

for captain. Just look how he had stepped in to help decide that call. And if everyone else wanted him to be captain, who was Dewey to mess that up by entering the contest?

# Chapter 4

**O**n the sideline, Amanda prepared to throw in. She took the ball in both hands, brought it back behind her head, and heaved.

The throw-in reached Stookie safely. He controlled it and began his attack.

Dewey held back and let Eddie and Lisa hound Stookie. He kept an eye on the action, though, ready to swoop in if Stookie got around them or tried to pass to Roy.

But Roy outsmarted him. He sneaked around Dewey and trapped a perfect pass from Stookie with his foot. Seconds later, he shot at the goal. Ted tried his hardest to stop it, but he was no goalie. The ball sailed between the posts for the first goal of the game.

Ted apologized to his team. "I sure hope our new team has someone to play goalie," he remarked to Dewey. "This position rots, if you ask me."

The rest of the pick-up game went by swiftly. The teams were pretty evenly matched, but in the end Bundy's group won, 3–2.

"Hey, Dewey," Bundy called as everyone started to head home. "Can you come by my house after lunch?"

"I guess," Dewey replied.

"Awesome," Bundy said. "I was hoping you'd tell me what you think of the logo I drew last night. I think it's pretty good."

*Oh, boy,* Dewey thought, his heart sinking. *What am I going to say if it's not?*

"Come on up," Bundy said when he opened the door. He led the way to his room.

Bundy was a real sports fan. He had posters, banners, and souvenirs from all kinds of teams on his walls. Dewey looked closely at the professional team logos. They were drawn with thick, bold lines that slashed through bright background colors. The animal ones seemed to be in motion.

Could Bundy possibly have created something as good as that? Dewey hoped so—but was pretty sure he hadn't.

Bundy pulled out a wrinkled piece of paper and held it against his chest.

"Before I show you my drawing," he said, "let me tell you how I came up with my idea." He started to pace. "Soccer is all about being powerful and lightning quick, right? So I thought, what about a fast, strong animal? Animals are cool." With a hopeful look, he handed his paper to Dewey.

Dewey's spirits sank. The drawing was awful—not much more than a squiggly black outline filled with black splotches and what might have been eyes. Dewey didn't have a clue what it was.

"Well, what do you think?" Bundy asked impatiently.

Dewey cleared his throat. "Um, I'm speechless."

Bundy took the paper back. "Yeah, I'm surprised at how good it came out, too," he said, looking at his drawing with satisfaction. "I mean, I just barely passed art last year. And now here I am, designing our team's logo! Can you believe it?"

*No*, Dewey thought dismally.

"So, you like the claws?" Bundy asked.

"Claws?"

Bundy rolled his eyes. "Well, duh, what did you think those things at the ends of its paws were? Rubber bands?" He started laughing.

"Paws?" Dewey repeated stupidly. Then he thought of the black splotches. Quickly, he tried to remember what animal had claws,

black dotted fur, and was known for its speed and power. "It's a — cheetah?" he guessed.

Bundy rolled his eyes. "Obviously. It's a cool name, isn't it?"

Dewey nodded. But at the same time, he imagined himself wearing a T-shirt with that drawing. He shuddered.

"So you like it?" Bundy asked.

Everything in Dewey wanted to tell Bundy that the drawing was no good. Bundy still had time to draw another one, but would that one be any better? Dewey didn't think so.

But he had to say *something*.

"Uh, maybe you should add in a soccer ball somewhere," he suggested lamely.

"Yeah!" Bundy cried. "I knew I could count on you — you're way better at art than I am." He shook his head. "You know, I still can't believe you're not going to enter the contest yourself."

Dewey mumbled something about not wanting to compete with Bundy.

Bundy grinned. "That's why it's so great you're not entering, because you'd win for sure." He punched Dewey lightly on the arm. "Thanks, buddy."

Dewey gave him a weak smile.

# Chapter 5

**W**hen Dewey came home from Bundy's house, his mother handed him a letter. He tore it open.

"It's the soccer schedule," he reported. He quickly scanned the letter. "Our first practice is Monday afternoon, and our first game is Friday. Our team T-shirt color is yellow."

"Yellow's a good color," she commented.

*Yeah,* Dewey thought. *Just right for a cheetah. Oh, boy.*

"You should put that schedule in a safe

place," his mother advised. "In case you forget when a game is."

Dewey nodded and hurried upstairs to put the letter in his desk drawer. He was about to stuff the letter inside when he saw the crinkled rule sheet.

He stared at it, then slowly pulled the paper out and read through it.

The rules were pretty simple. You came up with a team name, drew a logo to go with it, and submitted it to your coach. The team members voted on the one they liked best. If yours was chosen, you'd be team captain and your drawing would be put on your team T-shirts. The T-shirts became the team uniforms.

On top of Dewey's desk was the special sketch pad his father had given him after he'd won the art prize. *Maybe I'll just sketch out a few ideas,* Dewey thought. *Just for fun.*

He tipped back in his chair, chewing on the

end of his pencil. He thought about the sports teams he knew: the Red Sox, the Yankees, the Marlins. The Pistons, the Bulls, the Jazz. The Cowboys, the 49ers, the Lions.

*Lions! Lions are fast and ferocious,* he mused. *Bundy had the right idea about choosing an animal for the logo, anyway. I'll try drawing a lion.*

He started to sketch. Fine, flowing lines made the mane. The eyes were fierce. He drew the mouth so that the razor-sharp teeth showed. The body looked muscular, with four sturdy legs planted firmly on the ground.

When he was finished, he sat back and looked at his drawing. It was a good picture of a lion. But somehow, it wasn't right.

He thought back to Bundy's room and the team logos he'd seen there. His lion was good, but it looked like something you'd see in an encyclopedia. Not very exciting.

He tore the sheet off the pad, wadded it up, and threw it away.

Half an hour later, he'd added three more sheets to the trash can. His lions were all fine, but they just weren't . . . inspired.

*Guess I can't draw a logo any better than Bundy can,* Dewey thought. *It's probably just as well. I mean, what was I going to do, enter the contest? Ha!* He put the sketch pad aside, tucked the rule sheet in with the schedule letter, and left his room.

# Chapter 6

On Monday, the day of the first practice, Dewey and Bundy walked together to the soccer field. The members of Team Six were milling about. Along with the kids from the pick-up game were a few kids Dewey knew on sight: Brant Davis, a short African-American boy with a sharp buzz cut; Bucky Pinter, who stood almost as tall as Lou; and Jason Shearer, a wisecracking kid who always seemed to be chewing gum.

A whistle shrilled. Dewey spun around to

see a tall man with sandy brown hair. He looked about thirty years old and was in good shape. Under each arm was a soccer ball. In one hand he held a clipboard.

"Hi, everyone. I'm Don Bradley. You can call me Coach." Coach Bradley dropped the soccer balls and took a quick roll call. Then he tossed the clipboard aside. "Okay, enough of that nonsense. Let's get to playing some soccer, huh?"

"Yeah!" all the kids cheered enthusiastically.

"How many of you have played before?" the coach asked.

Everyone raised their hands.

"Great!" Coach Bradley said enthusiastically. "Then I'm going to do something a little unorthodox, okay?"

The kids looked at one another uncertainly.

"What does *unorthodox* mean?" Alan whispered to Ted.

"I dunno," Ted mumbled back.

Jerry Dinh stuck his head in between them. "I think it means he's going to do something someone else might not do."

"Right," Coach Bradley's voice cut in. "Most of the other coaches are probably putting their teams through boring drills." He made snoring noises. "There's plenty of time for that another day. Today, I'm going to break you into two teams so we can scrimmage. Since there are fifteen of you, we'll play seven-on-seven, and someone can help me referee."

Dale volunteered to ref. Coach Bradley split the rest of the team into two groups.

"Let's have a two-two-two lineup with one player in goal," Coach Bradley continued. "Okay, who likes to play what?"

Moments later, the lineup for one team was Lou and Roy at striker, Dewey and Eddie at halfback, and Brant and Alan at fullback.

"Looks like I'm in the hot seat," Jason

Shearer remarked as he hustled to that team's goal position.

Bucky Pinter went more eagerly to his team's goal. His fullbacks were Ted and Lisa Gaddy. The halfbacks were Bundy and Amanda, and Jerry and Stookie filled the striker slots.

Coach Bradley tossed a ball to Dale. "Go get 'em started, ref," he said. "Jerry, why don't you take the kickoff?"

Dale placed the ball in the center circle at Jerry Dinh's feet, and the scrimmage started.

Jerry tapped the ball to Stookie. Stookie dribbled a few feet, then passed back to Jerry. Lou stuck a foot in to steal, but Jerry powered his way past him.

But Eddie and Dewey weren't about to let him just waltz on by. Together, they attacked.

Jerry panicked. The ball squirted free, and Lou Barnes picked it up. His long legs covered a lot of ground. In a flash, he was in front of the Gaddy twins, looking to take a shot on goal.

Lisa and Ted swarmed on him. But Lou was too powerful. He dodged by them and fired a kick directly at the goal.

*Whap!*

Bucky Pinter leaped and slapped the ball down. No goal!

Lou looked shocked that he hadn't scored.

Coach Bradley retrieved the ball. "Looks like I got myself a goalie!" he yelled. "Okay, since Bucky knocked it out of bounds over the goal line, Lou's team gets to take a corner kick. Dewey, you take it."

Dewey hurried over to the small quarter-circle in the corner of the field. He waited until his team was in position and the other team had backed up the required ten yards. Then he booted the ball toward the area in front of the goal.

Roy deflected the kick perfectly. This time, Bucky couldn't stop it. Goal!

As Bucky kicked at the ground, Dewey and his team cheered loudly. Then everyone hustled back to their starting positions, and play resumed.

Back and forth the game went. Dewey made some good plays, including a steal that left Stookie Norris standing with his mouth wide open — and ended with Lou Barnes making a goal.

"You were like a cat, the way you pounced on that ball," Bundy commented as he passed Dewey. "Or should I say, like a cheetah?" He waggled his eyebrows and grinned.

Dewey returned the grin, but suddenly his mind was spinning. Something Bundy had said had made an image pop into his head. He could see it now: a wildcat pouncing on a soccer ball, paws outstretched, eyes fierce, teeth bared. If he could get the angle just right, he'd make the cat look like it was leaping right off the page.

He knew he could draw it and that it would be the perfect logo. He couldn't wait for practice to end so he could go home to his sketch pad.

# Chapter 7

When the score was tied at 3–3, Coach Bradley blew his whistle to gather the team together.

"Good game, everyone," he praised. "The positions you chose for yourselves seem to fit, so we'll stick with them for now." Coach Bradley ignored the groan that came from Jason Shearer. "We've got fifteen minutes left, so let's run some laps."

He held up his hand as the kids started to moan. "You can bellyache all you want, but think about this. Our first game is four days away. Do you want to be out of breath for it, or in shape?" He let that sink in, then added, "If it'll make you feel better, I'll run with you." The kids let out a cheer as he took off his whistle and started them out around the field.

Dewey was breathing hard by the time they finished their laps. Just before the team broke practice for the day, Coach Bradley made an announcement.

"Those of you who are entering the logo contest, entries are due the day of the game. We'll judge them after we win." He grinned.

Bundy winked at Dewey and raised his hand. "What if we only have one person entering? Do we still have to judge?"

Coach Bradley stroked his chin. "Well, if that's the case," he said, "we'll just get a preview of our team logo instead. All right, see you all tomorrow."

Dewey and Bundy left together. Dewey hoped Bundy would talk about the practice instead of the contest. But his hopes were dashed just as they reached Bundy's house.

"Can't wait to show my logo on Friday," Bundy said. "You're sure it looks good, right?"

*Now's your chance!* the voice in Dewey's head cried out. *Tell him it stinks and that you've come up with a better idea!*

"Yo, earth to Dewey!" Bundy tapped on Dewey's head. "Are you okay?"

Dewey forced a smile. "Just tired, I guess. Those laps took it out of me. Think I'll head home and hit the shower."

Bundy shrugged. "Good idea. That'll take care of that odor problem of yours." Laughing, he said good-bye and stepped into his house. Dewey continued on home, feeling like a traitor every step of the way.

Then he thought of something.

*I haven't actually drawn the picture yet. Maybe it'll stink as bad as my lions did.*

Feeling a little better, he jogged the rest of the way home.

# Chapter 8

His picture didn't stink. Dewey worked on it from supper until bedtime. When he was through, it was perfect, just as he'd imagined it on the field that day.

Yet Dewey couldn't look at it with satisfaction. How could he, knowing he'd gone behind his best friend's back?

Before he turned out the light, he made up his mind. He was going to come clean with Bundy. He had to—because Bundy would find out soon enough, after the game on

Friday, when Dewey submitted his wildcat drawing.

Dewey didn't sleep very well that night. But the next morning, he stuck to his decision. He called Bundy right after breakfast and told him the news.

The silence on the other end of the phone was deafening. Dewey leaned his head back against the wall, waiting for Bundy to say something. Anything.

"Well, Dewey," Bundy said at last, "I guess I'll have to call you Captain from Friday on." His voice was thick with disappointment.

"Bundy—," Dewey started to say.

"What I don't get," Bundy interrupted, "is why you weren't up front with me about wanting to be in the contest right from the start. I mean, you said over and over that you didn't want to be captain!"

"I don't," Dewey said miserably.

Bundy made a choking sound. "So what's

the deal? Why won't you let me be the only one to enter?"

Dewey sighed. "I don't want to hurt your feelings, Bundy. But you drawing, well, it's no good. I couldn't even tell what it was at first."

Bundy was quiet for so long, Dewey thought he'd hung up. Then Bundy said, "Well, thanks, Dewey, thanks a lot."

Dewey heard a strange ripping sound.

"Don't worry, Mr. Artist, I just tore up my drawing. Now you won't ever have to look at it again."

Dewey tried to say something, but Bundy wasn't finished.

"And I'll tell you what. Maybe my drawing is lousy. But you're going to make a lousy captain!" Bundy slammed the phone down.

Dewey put the phone back in the cradle slowly. He trudged up to his room and lay on his bed, staring at the wildcat drawing. He wanted to rip it up and tell Bundy that he

wasn't going to enter the contest either. But Dewey figured Bundy wasn't likely to try drawing another logo—not after what Dewey had said about his cheetah picture.

*Man,* thought Dewey. *This stupid contest. Why can't I be the one to draw the logo and Bundy be the one to be captain?*

Dewey blinked. He sat up.

"Wait a minute," he said out loud. "Why didn't I think of this before?"

He rummaged through his desk drawer, pulled out the soccer letter, and picked up the phone. He dialed a number. When the person on the other end picked up, Dewey identified himself, then asked, "I wonder, would it be okay if I did something, um, unorthodox?"

# Chapter 9

It was the day of the first game. Team Six showed up in their bright yellow T-shirts. Team Four wore dark blue.

Coach Bradley called his team together. Dewey tried to catch Bundy's eye, but Bundy ignored him.

"Okay, we're playing a three-three-four lineup," Coach Bradley reminded them. "Lou, Jerry, and Stookie are strikers. In halfback position, left to right, we've got Dewey, Bundy, and Amanda. At fullback, it's Brant, Lisa, Ted, and Alan. Bucky, you're my goalie."

He looked at the disappointed faces of those not named. "Just so you know, everyone will always play every game. That's a promise." The faces brightened.

Coach Bradley continued, "Let's remember the basics. Everyone stay in their lanes. Don't bunch up around the ball. You're not bees swarming a flower, after all." He waited until the kids had stopped laughing. "Take good shots on goal, and don't hog the ball." He tapped his chin. "Let's see, what else? Oh, yeah. Have fun! Let's hear it, now!"

The kids stuck their hands in a circle and gave a whoop.

Team Six had possession first.

When the whistle blew, Jerry quickly toed the ball to Lou. Lou took off down the sidelines. Dewey was behind him all the way.

It was a good thing he was, because Lou got stripped. But the Team Four striker made a bad dribble. Dewey swooped in and snared

the ball from her. A quick boot sent it sailing to Jerry.

Jerry passed just as quickly to Stookie. Stookie sped downfield with a full head of steam. Dewey was pretty sure he was going to try a shot on goal.

He did—but it missed by a mile and bounced harmlessly over the goal line. The referee retrieved it and handed it to the goalie. The goalie put it on the ground in the goal area and kicked it high and far. It landed at midfield.

Bundy, Amanda, and Jerry rushed to it, as did three players from Team Four. Bundy got to it first. After a quick glance at Dewey, he passed to Lou. Once again, Lou galloped downfield with the ball.

He made it farther than he had before, but not close enough to the goal for a good shot. A Team Four halfback intercepted his pass to Jerry and sent the ball rocketing over Dewey's head.

The Team Four right striker stopped it on her chest. When it fell to the ground, she shot it over to the center striker. Without a pause, the center booted it to the striker on his left.

But the left striker wasn't paying attention, so he missed the pass. The ball bounced over the sideline.

"Okay, Amanda," Dewey yelled. "Make the throw-in good!"

Amanda did. Jerry trapped it expertly. Within seconds, he had dodged around the defense and taken a shot on goal.

It was in! Team Six was on the scoreboard!

That was the only goal of the game. The two teams battled back and forth. Each came dangerously close to scoring, but neither did. When the final whistle blew, Team Six had registered its first win.

# Chapter 10

"Okay, gather round, Team Six!"

Coach Bradley's voice boomed happily over the field. The team had slapped "good game" hands with Team Four. Now they were gathered near their bench, slurping on orange slices and juice.

"I'll be glad not to have to keep calling you Team Six after today," Coach Bradley joked. "Now, down to business. We have only one entrant for the logo contest, which means the judging should be pretty quick."

All eyes swung to Bundy. But Bundy kept his head lowered and picked at some grass.

Coach Bradley produced his clipboard. With a grand gesture, he whisked a piece of paper from it and held it up for all to see.

"Wow!" said Amanda.

"Awesome!" echoed Dale.

"Look at those teeth!" exclaimed Alan.

"*Bundy* drew that?" said Jason, snapping his gum.

Coach Bradley smiled. "I take it you approve," he drawled. The kids all shouted yes. All except Bundy.

"But Bundy didn't draw this picture," said the coach.

The team was suddenly silent.

"The creator of your team name, the Soccer 'Cats, and the team logo is Dewey London. Dewey, could you stand up, please?"

Awkwardly, Dewey rose to his feet.

"*He's* going to be our captain?" Jason had

only whispered it, but Dewey heard him loud and clear. He was sure everyone else did, too. He flushed.

"Uh, actually, no," Dewey mumbled. Bundy's head shot up. He stared at Dewey.

"I never wanted to be captain," Dewey continued, his voice getting stronger. "I just like to draw, that's all." He paused, then fixed Bundy with a return stare.

"No one knows better than me who should be captain of this team. In fact, if it weren't for him, I wouldn't have even come up with the idea for the Soccer 'Cats." He explained about Bundy's comment during the scrimmage and how it had led him to getting the idea for the picture.

"So, in a way, it really is Bundy's logo. Which means he won the contest and should be captain," he finished.

"I second that!" Lisa Gaddy cried. The rest of the team cheered their agreement.

"Bundy, could you come up here, please?" Coach Bradley requested.

Bundy stood up and joined the coach and Dewey.

"Captain Neel," Coach Bradley said ceremoniously, "may I present you with the team logo, drawn by our own team artist?" He handed Bundy the paper.

"Wow," Bundy said, staring at the paper. "Dewey, you're the best." He smiled. "And I'm not just talking about how you draw, either."

Dewey grinned.

"Now, go home," Coach Bradley said, "and get those sweaty T-shirts washed and back to me by tomorrow — so I can make sure that the Soccer 'Cats' uniforms are ready for our next game!"